Rush Of Many Waters

Also by Pauly Hart

Novels:
By the Gates of the Garden of Eden
Novellas:
Superior Respondent
Ouesso to Epena
The Book of Lesser Voices
Mountain to Mountain
The Word of Yahweh unto Enoch
Empire of the Dragon
Finance:
The Richest Man In Babylon Continued Stories
Collections:
Sometimes I Write Tiny Stories
Adelphoi
Poetry:
Stupid Mind Tricks
Book of Love and Laughter
The Cross and the Poet
What is Poep?
I Love You More Than a Fox Loves Blueberries
The Night Clerk Held a Broken Pencil
Spontaneous Psalms
Kick the Prick
Exegesis with Co-Authors:
My Flat Earth
Biblical Cosmology, 8+ languages
Translations:
The Testament of Job in Modern English
Children's:
Mathmagician and Other Tales of Awesomeness
Periodicals:
Modern Epistle (1-8)
Microzine (1-5)
Rush of Many Waters (1-20)
With children authors:
Farrell Family Fables
With Co-Author Jennifer Hart:
Adulting: A Daily Guide on Being an Adultier Adult
Audiobooks:
Biblical Cosmology
Superior Respondent

Rush of Many Waters:

Volume Eighteen

By Pauly Hart

Rush of Many Waters: Volume Eighteen

ISBN: 978-1-955399-21-0

Library of Congress Catalog Data is available at: Loc.gov

This book is available at cost on Amazon.com and wherever fine books are sold.

Front Cover Art by Franz Marc:

Front cover design by Pauly Hart

Paperback version printed in Savannah, Georgia, USA, where available.

First Edition, 2021

Author Contact: EmpiresAndGenerals@gmail.com

Author Website: PaulyHart.com

Contents

Shorts

Rain Bistro

It was late at night when Basil realized that he had forgotten his thermometer. It was a special thermometer, the one his mother had given him when he was only eight years old. He rushed back to work to get it. But work had already closed up for the day and the night watchman wasn't going to be in for another couple of hours. Not a large deal, he would just have to wait in the rain until he came in... Four hours.

It was getting dark and the little rain scaffold that was over the front of the building was not near enough protection from the elements to last four hours. There was a small deli around the corner about a block up. He would wait there. They were closed as well. It was seven o'clock. He had never been here this late and he had supposed them to just stay open all night. He rapped on the window to the man cleaning the floor. The man looked at him, pointed to his wrist (even though he was not wearing a watch) and continued cleaning the floor. Basil thought was rather rude, but the man paid him no heed when he rapped again.

At least they had a proper awning here where the rain couldn't reach him. It was going on eight but the night watchman wouldn't arrive yet until ten. He was very cold and wondered what there was around here to do while he waited. He was hungry and he was wet. The weather wasn't dreadfully cold and he could wait if he had to but he would rather do it inside. He picked up his bag and started out down the street. He had never walked down this way before and, since he had nothing better to do, it seemed like the right thing to do.

The right thing indeed. There was a restaurant just up ahead. How he had not noticed this before was somewhat of a small mystery to him. It looked nice, like an Italian Bistro. Nice dark wood inside with open rafters and plastic ivy hanging all around. They were open, but there were no customers. Two people in white shirts and black aprons sat at the bar, employees with nothing to do.

He noticed the hours on the door: "Open ‘til midnight, every day." That was odd. Usually places like this closed around ten didn't they? Never minding the sign, he opened up the door and walked in.

Liza had experienced flat tires before. Once when she was on a road trip to Summersville, she had to change one herself. But as she peered into the trunk of her little car she realized that the spare tire was flat as well. It didn't make sense but there was nothing to do about it. She was a member of AAA so she would just call them and wait. She shut the trunk and got back in the car and locked herself in. You couldn't be too safe. Not downtown at night. She had heard stories.

Her phone was conspicuously dead. Totally dead. Not a big deal. Her phone charger was in her purse. Oh. No it wasn't. It was still at home on the table next to her bed wasn't it? Well. The office was still open and she would call from there. Snap. The door from the parking garage was locked. She would have to walk down to another level and get in the elevator room and get in from there.

Down a flight and back to the elevator room. Locked. Another floor down and it was the same story. Her luck hadn't changed. It just hadn't gotten any better. She walked down to street level and tried the building's front door. Not so amazingly, it was also locked. She didn't work late very often but today had been an exception. She guessed she didn't know that the building would be locked. There was a man on the street with a bag walking with his head down in the rain. It seemed like a good idea to follow him and so, she did.

He was headed towards that little Bistro up the street. That was probably a good idea. Get out of this rain and have some coffee while she used their phone. He opened the door as she walked up.

Basil opened the door and found a woman behind him. He had just opened the door and found himself saying "After you," In a very polite manner. He followed in behind her and they stood there for a second adjusting to the interior of the restaurant. She was pretty and smiled at him and said: "Thanks."

One of the waiters slid off the stool and quickly walked over to them.

"Hi folks! Two tonight?" She asked.

Basil was at a loss for words and was about to say something like they had just randomly come in together but thought the better of it.

Sometimes you should just agree with people around you and let them direct your way. You never know what could come of it.

"Yes. Two for non-smoking," he said.

Both the woman and the waiter looked at him strangely.

"Ah, yes, we don't actually have a smoking section, so I can sit you anywhere," she began. "Would you like a booth or a table?"

"A booth if you please." Liza said.

Much is said of chance meetings. Fifteen years later they both looked back on that night with fondness. They never talked to each other and, eventually, each went their separate ways. Basil had tea and eventually got let in to the building to retrieve the thermometer. Liza, after coffee, had her car towed to a local shop and had gotten her home by around eleven. But they always remembered the fondness in the other's eyes over their hot drinks, on that cold and rainy night.

Olpec

It was the end of days, the last day of Olpec's job. There was nothing else to do but wait on the coordinator. The air smelled of burned hair and garbage. Plastic littered the battlefield and Olpec's cannon was smoldering. The broken arms of spider tanks lay around... Or were they legs? The broken tendrils of spider tanks lay around him, still twitching with residual programming. They were little beasts, to be sure. Although his twenty foot frame gave him plenty of room to maneuver, he had nothing on those little critters. They were only a foot high, but carried a .44 magnum mid-sized barrel that packed quite the wallop. He was dented, and in some cases the armor piercing rounds had gotten through his skin but he was still mostly functional. 88% was a pretty good number considering his odds.

There was an explosion off to his left. He swiveled in that direction and was disappointed to find that it was only one of the tankers that had brought the mini-tanks. Another explosion behind it, and another... Then four more all at once... Then nothing. Had they been on a timer of sorts or…? He scooped up one of the critters with his left lower arm and examined it. He popped the top off with a satisfying *kerwoosh*.

Oooh, he got it now. Each spider tank had an antenna built inside the top casing that was in communication with the tankers. There was no communication now obviously, but he reckoned that the tankers were programmed to detonate in case their army had been wiped out.

It made sense tactically. If it were his army, he wouldn't want his tech to fall into the hands of the enemy. There wasn't anything to steal intellectually. The coordinators had taken the Russian's entire tech long ago and found out everything there was to know. Well now, except for the antenna.

Oooh, he got it now. He didn't need to know about the communication, so they hadn't told him of course. He had only been programmed with the needs of the battle at hand. That made sense. It also made him feel a little hurt. They had trusted him enough to go out alone into the field, but they hadn't told him about their antenna. What else hadn't they told him about?

He was curious. He still had the spider tank in one of his hands so he popped open his scanpad from his lower torso and set the critter down on it. He would have to take his optics off-line but that wouldn't be a big deal. He still had his radar and motion-sensors active just in case. He ran a full scan and opened the results all at once. His CPU had 18 Teraflop of RAM so it could handle something like this with ease. The results were very interesting. The programming was simple enough, there were even options for air and sea tactics and strategy, but this model wasn't equipped with that hardware. This was land model 5.3 - assault build. The most versatile unit he supposed. But why would they send these guys to battle him?

Oooh, he got it now. They didn't know what they would be up against.

That was a shame. The battle hadn't been difficult in the least. Tedious to be sure but not difficult. Most of his time he just walked around strategically trying to squash as many as he could with each step. The rest of the time he was scraping them off of his legs or shooting off mortars. He had used his static-field only twice when a couple of them got on his head, but mostly he had been too quick for them. It had been too easy. The model on his scanpad had a "name" too but it wasn't a name a caring coordinator would give. 0583733-CLTY-522.

Oooh, he got it now. There were so many of them that proper names would be too confusing. How sad. Were there more than 583,000 of them? Or was he 522 of the assault force? Most probably both. He decided that 0583733-CLTY-522 needed a better name. The most obvious choice would be to use the middle alpha characters. The consonants determined that he should add a vowel between the "C" and the "L." He chose "O" for Colty.

Hello little Colty. Nice to meet you.

Olpec had never met anyone before. Of course Colty was dead, so maybe it didn't count. The coordinators were just implanted memories of course. And they didn't use actual voices, they had just spelled out the battle plan and told him about how the Russians were bad and they were going to try and kill him and he needed to stop them. Of course he would stop them. That was his purpose. That was his mission. Stop the Russians. And he had. He was a good soldier.

He turned his optics back on and looked down at Colty. He didn't look so bad now that he was dead. As a matter of fact, even if Colty was alive he couldn't harm him because there was just one of him. All the other spider tanks with all of their guns hadn't stopped him, so how could Colty? He decided that he would repair him so he could say hello in person. Colty had been one of the many that had been crushed under Olpec's large feet. They were gloriously large indeed. Four feet in diameter with a toe on each of the four sides. He had three of them, unlike Colty's eight. Reattaching Colty's wires and circuits was very difficult because several of them had been crushed beyond repair. He was forced to scavenge among Colty's brothers to find the correct pieces.

When Colty came to life he shot him. He had tried to at least. *Click click click click click click click click click* went his gun. He scrambled up and down Olpec's frame clicking away angrily. He clicked forty-two times. Even though Olpec had emptied out his chamber, he knew Colty would run the programming that he was programmed to run.

"Hello Colty," Olpec said, "nice to meet you."

Colty did not care to meet Olpec evidently, for when it finally realized it was out of rounds, it scrambled up on top of Olpec's head and tried to pry his helmet off.

"That won't work Colty," Olpec said, "Not even ten of you could take that off."

Again, Colty did not care, and after several minutes when it realized it would not succeed, Colty exploded.

This did not damage Olpec, but instead, horrified him. He had seen the cross-wires that connected the servo-manipulator to the power core, and he had even seen the self-destruct code in the programming, but he had not reasoned that Colty would actually do it, even though he was programmed to. The sheer thought that anyone would self-destruct was so foreign to him that he had dismissed it into the realm of the impossible. Was it really in the code? He checked his own code. Then he wondered: If you live too long, do you gain the desire to self-destruct? Did he have that code? He checked again. No. He didn't have that code. But he checked again. His code had changed. Before where there was nothing about self-destruction, now there were questions. And now there were even questions about those questions. Did everything need to die?

Oooh, he got it now, it was because he was an artificial intelligence, so he didn't need to die. Everything else needed to die.

Olpec had been born yesterday. That was a long time wasn't it? How old was Colty? Does the desire to self-destruct come with age or is it just programmed into you? It wasn't programmed into him. Was it programmed into the coordinators? He didn't know, and the thought of it all really depressed him. He folded up his arms and went into power-down mode until the coordinators called.

He would help the coordinators self-destruct as well. He had plenty of time to wait.

Charleston and the dig

It wasn't life that drew him in, it was something else.

As I slipped deeper into the bottom of the program, I knew I had reached the point of no return. This area wasn't coded and there was nothing I could do about it. I was going to die unless I pushed through passed the bottom.

Life had been on the surface. The drive over the railing and onto the support structure of the bridge had been a gambit that was do or die. "Do or die." What an awful phrase. Of course everything was do or die, wasn't it? "Life is either a daring adventure or nothing at all," Helen Keller had once said. Obvious. How to survive market mania? Do or die. How to S.C.U.B.A.? Do or die. How to push passed the program into the black? Do or die. His lungs hurt.

Charleston's hand reached farther down, he could almost touch the grommet. It was as precious to him as the One Ring of Power that Tolkien had written about so famously... Except this grommet didn't symbolize some mythological necromancer, it was just a grommet - but where it was, was important. It was in the black. He went farther down. His flashlight, used for underwater repair, seemed to dim in the blackness as he continued. He let out a belch of air, just a little. Didn't want to give it all up, but it was too much pressure down here.

That's odd, he thought, but then countered with: Of course it won't work, it's not programmed to work. Not down here. All around him, the darkness was creeping in, like octopus ink, inside the water, making it all become blacker and blacker. It had taken him three minutes to get this deep. He only had two minutes left of air. His lungs were starting to cramp. Do or die.

Down, down, down, until he hit bottom. Bottom? The bottom of what? How could there be a bottom when no bottom was programmed? Oh, he realized. It's absolute zero. This is where there could be no programming. He felt the floor. With no light and no way to see what he was looking at, he thrust his hand into it. It was like the bottom of a real lake, soft, gooey, clay-like gum that moved easily with his movements. He thrust the flashlight into his belt, not bothering to turn if off, He dug. His lungs were on fire.

He had no way to gauge how far he had gotten when he felt his breath belch on it's own. He lost more air. It felt good, but now the impulse, or the instinct to breathe in had to be battled. Fool. There is only water to breathe in. You will die. Dig, dig, dig.

Charleston's eyes were burning, his heart hurt, his lungs were a molten magma, screaming at him that all was lost and to just give up... Yet through the sheer force of will he continued to dig into the floor of absolute zero. His body became a machine, working on it's own. Right hand in, scoop out, left hand in, scoop out, paddle down with both legs, dig, dig, dig... His mind wandered.

Trish was up there, probably, looking over the railing, crying. No. Trish would be screaming. Not having the fortitude to dive in herself, she would probably be holding her stomach with both arms, in a tortured hug, with that peach sun dress. The one with the frills on the sleeves. Like some throwback to 1965, all that was missing was a marigold in her hair. Marigolds. He hated those things. Like some... Wait... What was that? His hands told him something was happening.

He was digging in air. It wasn't muck, but with almost no resistance, he could feel himself going deeper, and there was light. Almost like daylight. The air was pudding, and he was falling.

When Charleston opened his eyes, he was in a field... And it was damned marigolds. Marigolds everywhere. He wasn't wet or dead. He was in a field filled with flowers. Or maybe he was dead and this was the great hereafter. Heaven? Hell? Purgatory? He didn't know.

A blinding flash sizzled before him and electricity shot around. A circle in the air opened and a man with a top-hat walked through the iris. After he came through, the blinding flash happened again and the circle sizzled close. The man with the top hat, dusted his jacket with his hand as if to get rid of some dust. He walked forward to Charleston and bowed.

Thurston Chamberson, at your service the man said.

Wow, what a pretentious name, Charleston thought.

Beg pardon? The man said.

Huh? Charleston said.

My name is just a name, the man said.

But I didn't say anything Charleston thought.

You can read minds? Charleston said.

Both correct, the man said. Here, there are no secrets.

Oh. Charleston thought, I must be in heaven.

No. Thurston said. You are just outside the program. This is free memory.

Poems

rape whistle

juni juniper lemons
wanted to be called edward
he had his game in two pieces
there was a sticker on it
must be paired with like-box
but the two boxes were paired
from two separate boxes
steve was there
edward wanted to impress steve
so as i came in
i mentioned that he should pair them with like-boxes
juni got mad
but
i was leaving
the summer festival was coming
i was dropping out in the spring
to go there early
instead of the fall like i did last year
i was in high spirits
i walked up the ramp to the cafeteria
i went in through the food chute
as i usually did on my shift
thelma had it blocked off
she apologized
she thought i had already left
we both laughed
i liked all the kitchen ladies
most of the kids didn't work there
the kitchen ladies were poor people
this was a school for rich kids
except me and steve

he had an athletic scholarship
i had an academic scholarship
i had on my good shoes
i was ready to leave
i said goodbye to all of them
i went down the hall to the principal's office
still some board members there
i casually knocked
almost
as i was about to knock
several of them came out
they came out laughing
in tweed jackets
horn rimmed glasses
they were getting another member of the board
it was almost official
one of them had passed on
a sudden stroke
on the golf course
why were they laughing
i left them all alone
snapping my fingers in the shape of a gun to his secretary
she said
we'll miss you
i took the stairs to the basement tunnel
the one that led from the admin to the dorms
the only tunnel at school
echos of someone yelling
juni was yelling for me
juni was singing for me
to the tune of:
do-do, do-do, do-doooooo-do
i knew what he would do-do
because it was what he was yelling
i'm going to rape your face!
in a sing song voice
echoing in the tunnel
but that's funny

because i knew he wouldn't touch me
i was leaving
no one touches people leaving
it's not done
you let them leave
they hold the grudge til next year
then i saw him
our eyes met
tiny watery blue inset eyes
the one of the left somewhat smaller
the one on the right somewhat crossed
he was a member of a medieval dress up club
they used foam weapons
juni had one in his hand
he had his foam greatsword
sewn into a colorful candy-cane fabric sleeve
he began to beat me with it
it did not hurt very much
but the wrath juni had
with the screaming
eyes red
saliva splattering
i could not move
...
face wrinkled with oil pouring down his forehead
sweat shaking from his hair
he was thrashing the shit out of me
with a foam weapon
once, then a scream
twice, then a scream
aweeeeeeah
he cried
it was seven or eight blows
people talking
coming down the staircase
from the main teaching building
hey what's this?
he shouted

the rage of juni
shook off like scared park pigeons
william, one of juni's friends from the club
william, the hall monitor
william also thought i was worthy of a beating
with him was steve
steve had been talking to william
now juni was in the presence of steve
steve who he wanted to impress
steve who threw quarterback touchdowns
juni could not throw
could not catch
was the biggest boy in school
but could not block steve in a blitz
had let steve down
but he stopped thrashing me
no one talked
william stopped asking questions
his job left his mind
suddenly he was just a mean boy again
whassamatter?
william asked
somebody raping you?
my glasses had fallen off
my water bottle was gone
i couldn't answer becau-
IS SOMEONE RAPING YOU?!
juni screamed at me
william screamed it too
steve feinted a laugh
kicked his foot nervously
he looked around
there was no one else there
steve looked back at me
tiny wrinkles appeared
his eyebrows grew closer
why don't you blow the rape whistle?
juni asked

of course william pushed it into my face
they had my head
william
juni
BLOW
BLOW
BLOW
into the whistle
they placed it into my mouth
BLOW
BLOW
BLOW
screaming
william grabbed it out of my hand
reached behind me
he rammed it up my behind
through my pants
WHY DON'T YOU BLOW IT OUT YOUR ASS
william hollered
they laughed
but then something inside juni snapped
something clicked
or
something fell into place
"yell rape"
juni said in a dull normal tone
there was a pause
i said nothing
"yell rape"
juni said again calmly
"do it"
he said
another pause
then
very slowly
he leaned into me
his warm hand gently on my neck
slowly pressing me back

fingers were meaty
palm was damp
pushing backwards
until i touched the wall behind me
shivers down my neck and arms
then pressed his fingers together
my saliva started flowing
pushing just a little more
"yell rape"
he said
"do it"
he said
little white spots in my vision
i could not say anything
i was watching his hair
there was a small bead of sweat
that had started near his hairline
run along a pimple on his forehead
down into his eye
where i thought it would have disappeared
but it collected more water
what looked like a tear
was not
it ran down his cheek
onto my arm
making the tiniest little splash
...
all that splash from such a tiny drop
...
i yelled rape
i yelled rape again
i closed my eyes hard
and again and again and again
i shrank to the floor
i grew louder and louder
screaming it
screaming it
at some point

like the teardrop
they splashed away
juni and william splashed away
then it was just me
on the floor
screaming incoherently
curled into a ball
wetting myself
...
...
...
eventually
...
it was just crying
...
eventually
it was just tears
with whimpers
...
eventually i was quiet
and shivering
and cold
and wet
and cramping
and silent
...
a woman screaming must have woken me
there was a lot of screaming
then more silence
was that the secretary?
footsteps
then more screaming by more people
i think it was boys this time
they also run away
i open my eyes on the floor
my view is of a trash can
someone threw paint all over it
all over the wall

paint everywhere
then running sounds
then more screaming
more adults
men
with hard hats
red hard hats
safety taped canvas clothing
picking me up
carrying me away
yelling things at me
...
so much noise after so much quiet
...
in an ambulance now
with more men
these have on white shirts with blue pants
they are closing the door
...
steve is there
right outside the door
he smiles
lifts a finger
to his lips
he smiles with his lips
his eyes do not smile
the door slams
we drive away

everywhere inside your shoes

i am only me
and where do i belong
i will look for you
even when you're gone
you are far away

i got your phone call yeah
oh when will you come home
please make it be today
i pray

everywhere inside your shoes
every time i'm feeling blue
i want you to come home to me
when i call to you, my daddy

the world seems awfully big
and i am awfully small
it's scary and i'm lost
but unto you i call
you are far away
i got your phone call yeah
won't you come out and play
'cause that would make my day
i know

i am scared and i am hurt
please come and save the day
i know you didn't mean it dad
but you left me in my pain

everywhere inside your shoes
everytime i'm feeling blue
i want you to come to me
when i call to you, my daddy

every step my daddy takes
is three steps for me
where were you when i was lost
when i was only three?

Find me

We were laying on the couch amidst the mess
You didn't care, you're laid your head upon my chest
And then you looked me in the eyes to my surprise
And tenderly you poked my face, and you said "mine"

My daddy (and then you cuddled up to me)
Sweet daddy (how i love you my dear Abby)

You were coming down the court on the full press
You passed and scored and my cheers did all the rest
But then you caught my eye, and to my surprise
You pointed straight at me, you told me you were mine

My daddy (when you cuddled up to me)
Sweet daddy (how i love you my dear Abby)

I was nervous at the pulpit i confess
But then the song played, my heart swelled in my chest
And you walked down the aisle, and you put your arm in mine
And you looked me straight in the eye... to my surprise... you said

My daddy (with you standing here next to me)
Sweet daddy (how i love you my dearest Abby)

I love you, you are mine
And I'll remember every time
that you called me what you called me:

My daddy.

Scarred Face

It's your saving grace
That comes over me
It's your loving face

That's all I see
It's your hiding place
That I run to

It's your love, your love, your love.

It's my face
That scares the children
It's my laugh

That makes them scream
It's my love
That makes me famous
It's my love, my love, my love.

I will come
To you my lover
I will come
To you tonight
I will climb in
To your garden

I will come, will come, will come.

No one could you like me
You cannot hide from me
I will come unto thee
When the night comes to the trees

Little Itty

Little Itty
Bitty Cat

Why oh why
did you pee on my hat?

Why wrestle shoestrings
Why eat the trash

You make me nervous
with your tiny claws

You frolic and wander
to seek and destroy

Itching and Scratching
My children's toys

Question and wonder
Meow, plead and beg

If you don't cut it out...
I'll... ouch, dammit!

Queer

'what was under the bed?'
he asked himself,
over and over...
all night long.

'what was in the closet?'
she asked herself,
under the covers...
all night long.

'what was in the basement?'
they asked themselves,
up in their rooms...
all night long.

probably something queer.

but they never found out,
because when morning came,
they went out to play,
because it was spring.

but it was something queer,
later that night.

definitely something queer.

Dance into the darkness

All the while I stood there waiting.
All the time you sat debating.
Would you ask me for a dance?
You did not even cast a glance.

I died for you in your place.
I cried at your sinful disgrace.
So I get shoved now out of the way.
I see your promise fade into gray.

I've given all and still I give.
You've taken all and yet you live.
Apart from me, no care, no plea.
No need you ever see for me.

I'll cry all day you've lost the way.
I'll curse the day you disobeyed.
For even though I know you well.
That blatant sin sends you to hell.

"Father" I beg, "Have mercy please".
"On those refusing to dance with me".

"Cast them not out to the left".
"Father" I cry, "Your sheep I've kept!"

(Dream on you fool while ice grows hard.
Bridging their hearts into the dark.
Dark chasms yell tormenting screams.
On fallen children I will feed!)

I'm 53

I'm fifty-three and scared,
remembering Vietnam.
I know that's where they took me,
to the concentration camp.

My birthday is on Tuesday,
just like it was back then.
I look back and remember.
that Charlie didn't care.

I was twenty-three and scared,
remembering back home.
My Father was the preacher,
of a small town Baptist church.

He told me life was precious,
He said: "Hang on to God.".
He preached that when things got bad,
God would take your hand.

I'm fifty-three and scared,
but God still lives in me.
That is what saved my soul,
when I was twenty-three.

Lord, you are Lord

Lord guide me
Surely hide me
make me an instrument
submitted to you

Lord Guide me
In your heart hide me
Take all my emptiness
And fill me with you

You alone, You are Lord
Upon the highest of the Heavens
You alone, You are Lord
Above the Cherubim

And Oh Lord, We'll Worship You
From the Beginning to the end of time
You exist, and Lord you reign
Above creation

Take my heart, Lord take my hands
And do with me what you will
You're my God, You are my King
Now and forevermore

Most Holy Lord, You are my Lord
My heart longs after none other
Lord, You alone, You are my Lord
And I will worship you

Spontaneous Psalm #1

Help me cause I'm slipping

I look to Jesus
When I see lies and tribulation
When I see the veil rip from heaven

I look to Jesus
He's always there
Look to Jesus
Cause I know he cares

And I know my life is over
When I lose him
I hope it never happens
I know my life would be without reason
To go on when he's gone

Don't leave me Jesus
Don't leave me my Savior
Cause I got nowhere to go

And I cry these tears
All these many years
And I go on
Just like the sun
Around the earth

So don't leave me Jesus
Cause I've got no one
Nobody to help me along this path
Besides you
Besides you

And I cry the cry of the pentitent
And I pray the prayers of the fervent
But what good does it do without you
What good is all of my life
When it comes down to
Not having you

And I cry the cry of the pentitent
And I pray the prayers of the fervent
But what good does it do without you
But what good does it do
If I had lost you

Make a river with these tears
For those who have ears to hear:
I have not left my Jesus
I will not leave my Savior
Though I drown in pain
And though I have nothing else to gain

And I cry the cry of the pentitent
And I pray the prayers of the fervent
But it does not mean a thing
If I lose you
But it does not mean anything to those
Which are without you

The cry of the pentitent
I pray the prayer of the fervent

Essays

Truth in the Valley

In February of 1995, my wife and I were in the coffee shop business. It had been a rough transition for the both of us, being recently married and just having moved into our new house. It is a story in itself of how we acquired the coffee shop, and how we envisioned it as a soul-saving shop for Jesus. Well, as it turned out, unequipped and untrained for this kind of venture, we landed on troubled times. We grew apart and our marriage was on the rocks. Unwilling to keep the commitment, we separated and I kept the coffee shop going.

So there I was, supposedly running a Christian coffee house with an eminent divorce looming over me. Neither my wife or I was nice to the other, and we were no example of the love we professed Christ to have. The house that we had purchased, we were forced to sell back to the realtor and eventually I closed the coffee shop. During that time, I had two of my best friends die of drug related misuse, my step-mother and my remaining grandfather died. Shortly thereafter, I totaled my car, almost killing two people in the process. Let me tell you the truth… I was in the valley of darkness.

In the book of the Psalms, Chapter eighty four, Verses five thru seven; the sons of Korah write about being in the valley. "Blessed is he whose strength is in (The Lord), whose heart is set upon the pilgrimage. As they pass through the valley of Baca, they make it a spring… They go from strength to strength until each one appears before God in Zion."

"Baca" in Hebrew means brokenness, or in other words the lowest time in their life. The lowest of the low. The uttermost. I was defiantly there in that time in my life. I had come into the valley of weeping. I had made it a spring with my tears. My valley was my life. It was all that I knew. I knew nothing else but pain at that time in my journey. I thought I would stay at that point for the rest of my life. I didn't see the way out of the valley. I figured that I was stuck there. However...

Oh how I love "howevers"!

However, my heart was set on the pilgrimage. My strength was in Him. I honestly can say that I did not have any surplus of strength to divvy out to any of my friends, but I did have my strength in Christ. All I had was in him. There was only one bright speck on my horizon, and that was Jesus Christ himself.

Have you ever heard Church people talk about going on from glory to glory? Have you ever seen in your life where you are going from strength to strength? To find out if this is real strength and real glory, you should be looking for the valleys. Oh it is hard to be going through those valleys, but remember what it was like before the valley. It will be good again after this valley. Is there a low point before the high point? There has to be... We go from strength to strength until we all appear before God in Zion.

Life will always have its ups. When my wife and I first started the coffee shop we had so much fun, there was excitement and the thrill was in the air. It was great! But life also has its valleys. My dearest reader, you would do well to remember that in each valley, Christ is there. Or have you forgotten Davids twenty third Psalm? It goes something like this:

"Even though I walk thru the valley of the fear of death, I won't be afraid, because you are with me! You are with me in my pain. You make me lie down and enjoy your presence. You fulfill me even in my pain. Surely goodness and mercy will relentlessly pursue me every day of my life and I will live in your house forever, Oh Lord."

Wow. What a promise. To have God be at the end of the quest. To know that no matter what baptism of pain you may be going through, He is there. Waiting, waiting, waiting... until... ZAP! Mercy comes in and floods your soul, and there is is the light at the end of the tunnel. Your ship comes in. Your life has meaning.

ZAP! Glory to glory!

ZAP! Goodness and mercy!
ZAP! Appearing before God in Zion!
ZAP! Dwelling in the house of the Lord forever!

myself on asian literacy

the dewy decimal system is at work in books that are in alpha-numerical order according to prefix and author and little ladies sitting behind old wooden desks with glasses on the end of their nose so do i feel a sense of history or just a minor attack of claustrophobia perhaps it is the old card system being replaced with the computer terminals or maybe it is the cd and video tape section that you can check out now i checked out a mandarin chinese audio teaching lesson once and copied it so i could learn all about how to speak the language but then i never got around to learning anything so i just ended up taking them back and checking out something else but even then i never have used them oh well i tell myself ill use it someday soon like perhaps when i go to china but ive heard stories about china like every book and especially each bible that is printed up has to be approved by the government and if its not then a prison term could follow do you know what ive heard about china as well is that in some parts of the country they dont have libraries and do you know what i think i said to myself i think ill have to pray about that

I will not!

I will not be the blessed of God if I don't follow the known will of God. I must and should be consecrated. I must take that awful and dreadful sword of the Lord and cut away everything that doesn't pertain to His will. I have to realize that I can miss Gods will by missing His timing. God! If I cannot have your will then take my life! Lord, if I don't get Your will and I get to Heaven and You tell me I didn't do Your will... I'll tell You that it's your fault; because THIS DAY I give you full permission to rebuke me, chastise me, correct me, and anytime you feel like it... you can tell me when I'm wrong.

And I'll obey.

This small life

Lands we will reach as we sail away but I don't want to let this life pass by. But how can we go anywhere when we don't have the courage to leave our homes? There was a bundle of blue yarn sitting on the desk next to me as i thought. Will my life amount to a hill of beans, or will I suffer in ignorance like the rest? My cute black puppy knows its purpose in its small miserable life, why don't I? People riding the busses, people working hard, driving the busses for them. Destinations posted on the front of the bus illuminating the marquee. I will season my thoughts over my heart and season it like some dry jerky. For it is been drained like from some sick hemomaniac. Heart sucked dry. We hold on to the most insane of ideas. We try too hard. We struggle. Like unto a mudskipper who believes it is his time to evolve are we. It won't be easy, it might be tricky, but we can't give up, we won't give up. This small life we partake of... Can the Madams or Psychic Friends help us? They can not evolve us... Who can add height or depth to himself by worrying? This small life we dream of is lost on the chords of some celestial guitarist. Does anyone know who we really are, or where this ghost train is taking us? The fog that we travel through, on our way to oblivion, Mother Mary help us. We struggle and strive and dream and sweat and eventually have our hearts sucked. Like as unto by some craven necrophiliac, as we lie in our tombs, we are abused. This small life is surrounded by darkness, except for that one small shaft of light. The light of Christ. The promise of the Jews and the hope of the Gentiles is He.

My shaft of light. My hope. My way. All the way my Savior will guide and help me through my small, so small life. And He will lead me to the bus station of my destiny.

Empires and Generals

One day, as I was minding my own business researching the Baalbek stones I came upon a new idea for a card game. I quit saponification immediately and started to work on Empires and Generals. *The world's first print-and-play free historical card game.* I put out an ad on The Pirate Bay and soon had over half a million viewers. It was shocking and wonderful all at the same time. That was in 2010 and the game is still going strong today. The point of the game was to allow children to learn real history that wasn't watered down by governmental authorities in a way that they would enjoy. Secondarily, it was to provide a collectible card game that wouldn't cause players to go bankrupt.

I created the game and set about to make hundreds and even today, thousands of new cards. I created an empire map of the entire world from 4134 BC until 1910 AD. My goal was to cover everything ever made or recorded militarily and culturally within the entire frame of the history of the earth and turn it into an accurate card game. Daunting. But it did give me cause to start watching crazy videos and researching historical oddities all at the same time. I am not a fan of revisionist history. It's wrong, it's evil, it's contrary to truth, I don't like it, and I believe that God would call it: "bearing a false witness."

Through my research in the game, I was able to find out many interesting things that have been hidden from the masses; probably the most interesting was giants. Giants, the Nephilim, ancient structures and pyramids... These things interested me more and more deeply. And the more and more I became interested in them, the more and more I found out about their world view. Their ancient calendars pointed towards the earth as the center of the universe. Their ancient clocks pointed towards a sun that rotated around the earth's surface. Their history, their common ancestors, and even the great deluge all pointed towards a Bible that taught that the earth was a plane, rounded and squared, and that had been one land mass at one time, but was now divided. In other words, the more history I learned, the more I became convinced that they knew the earth was flat. All of this thanks to a card game.

www.ingramcontent.com/pod-product-compliance
Lightning Source LLC
LaVergne TN
LVHW050951080826
845145LV00004B/1463
* 9 7 8 1 9 5 5 3 9 9 2 1 0 *